SUPERNATURAL RUBBER CHICKEN™

Poultry in Motion

By
D.L. Garfinkle

Illustrated by
Ethan Long

MIRRORSTONE

Poultry in Motion
Supernatural Rubber Chicken
Text ©2008 D. L. Garfinkle
Illustrations ©2008 Wizards of the Coast

Published by Wizards of the Coast, Inc.

Mirrorstone, Supernatural Rubber Chicken , and their logos are trademarks of Wizards of the Coast, Inc., in the U.S.A. and other countries.

Printed in the U.S.A.

Art by Ethan Long
Book designed by Yasuyo Dunnett and Kate Irwin

First Printing

9 8 7 6 5 4 3 2 1

ISBN: 978-0-7869-5013-3
620-21862740-001-EN

Library of Congress Cataloging in Publication Data

Garfinkle, D. L. (Debra L.)
    Poultry in motion / D. L. Garfinkle ; illustrated by Ethan Long.
        p. cm. -- (Supernatural rubber chicken)
    "Mirrorstone."
    Summary: The unusual and unexpected happens when Ed, the magical
rubber chicken that lives with ten-year-old twins Nate and Lisa,
misunderstands the wish Lisa makes for one of her classmates.
    ISBN 978-0-7869-5013-3
    (1. Magic--Fiction. 2. Wishes--Fiction. 3. Friendship--Fiction. 4 Twins--Fiction.
5. Brothers and sisters--Fiction. 6. Humorous stories.)
    I. Long, Ethan, ill. II. Title.
    PZ7.G17975Po 2008
    (Fic)--dc22
                                                    2008013172

U.S., CANADA,
ASIA, PACIFIC, & LATIN AMERICA
Wizards of the Coast, Inc.
P.O. Box 707
Renton, WA 98057-0707
+1-800-324-6496

EUROPEAN HEADQUARTERS
Hasbro UK Ltd
Caswell Way
Newport, Gwent NP9 0YH
GREAT BRITAIN
Save this address for your records.

Visit our web site at **www.mirrorstonebooks.com**

To my super sweet sister, April Holland

.• Contents •.

Fowl Language

Starring...

Chapter 1

Incredible but True: Someone Actually Wants to Go to School

"Please, please, please! For the love of all that is good and feathery, take me to school with you," Ed begged Lisa.

Ed was the rubber chicken owned by Lisa and Nate Zupinski.

Lisa and Nate Zupinski were ten-year-old twins who lived in Boring, Arizona. The Zupinskis were humans, not chickens. (However, Hulk Paine called Nate a chicken just last week because Nate wouldn't fight with him. Given that Hulk Paine was half a foot taller than Nate, fifty pounds heavier, and ten times as mean, Nate was smart not to fight him.)

But where were we?

Ah, yes.

At the moment, Ed the rubber chicken was on Lisa Zupinski's pink gingham bedspread, shouting, **"I want to go to school!"**

You might wonder how a rubber chicken could be shouting. This is how: **LOUDLY.**

Ed was supernatural. For one thing, he could talk. He was fluent in English, Spanish, and Swahili. He also knew a little Korean and Hungarian, and how to say "Get your filthy goat away from my pita bread" in Greek.

The only people who could hear Ed talk were his owners. (Lisa and Nate Zupinski, in case you weren't paying attention.)

The coolest thing about having a supernatural rubber chicken was that Ed could grant superpowers to anyone besides his owners. (If you still don't remember that Lisa and Nate Zupinski were his owners, then you *really* weren't paying attention. **WAKE UP!**)

Now where were we again?

Ah, yes. Ed asked Lisa, "You don't think I'm good enough to hang out with at school?"

Lisa peered down at the rubber chicken. "Why don't you ask my brother to bring you?"

"Nate?" Ed said. "He's a nice kid, but his

backpack is disgusting. Last time he put me in that thing, the horrible stink almost made me pass out. Just yesterday, I saw him put really gross stuff in there—used tissues, moldy strawberries, and a rat skeleton he found on the sidewalk."

"Eww," Lisa said.

"So will you take me to school with you?" the rubber chicken asked again.

"You forgot the magic word," Lisa said.

"Please?" Ed said.

"Yep." Lisa patted him on the head. "*Please* is the magic word all right."

"Great!" Ed exclaimed.

"But I can't take you to school," Lisa told him. "It's not that I don't like you. It's just that you'd clash with my outfit. A new girl is joining our class today. I want to make a good impression on her." Lisa smoothed the bottom of her dress. "This violet dress would look awful with a yellow rubber chicken in my arms."

"Put me in your backpack then," Ed pleaded. "Just leave the zipper open so it won't be too dark and scary in there."

"I have a lovely bedroom you can stay in today," Lisa said. "It's not dark or scary."

"Your bedroom may be lovely, but I get lonely in there," Ed said. "Your mom is the only one home all day, and she's always on her computer."

Lisa rolled her eyes. "Tell me about it."

"Okay," Ed said. "She uses the computer to write books."

"I didn't mean for you to really tell me about it. It's just an expression," Lisa said.

"Please take me with you today," Ed begged. "When you and Nate are at school, the only attention I get is from your dog, Plop. She licks me. Yuck! Plop's tongue has been

in the toilet. I don't want it on my face." Just talking about the dog's toilet-tinged tongue made Ed gag a little. "Please take me to school, Lisa. Please, please, please?"

Lisa sighed. "All right. Just don't cause any trouble."

"Me? Cause trouble?" the rubber chicken said. "Never!"

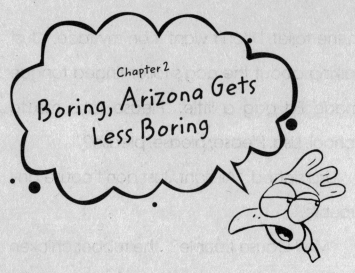

Chapter 2
Boring, Arizona Gets Less Boring

Nate and Lisa got off the school bus with Ed in Lisa's backpack.

Nate rushed to the handball court, where his best friend, Benny B. Benjamin, was waiting for him.

Lisa went to talk to her best friend, Ashley Chang. Actually, she went to listen to Ashley Chang. When Lisa was around Ashley, she didn't get much chance to talk.

"I wonder what that new girl will be like," Ashley said.

"Hopefully—" Lisa started to say.

"Hopefully, she'll be nice," Ashley interrupted her. "And fun to be around. With a good sense of humor."

"And—"

"And smart enough to help us study for Mrs. Crabpit's hard tests," Ashley said.

"I wonder—" Lisa tried again.

"Me too," Ashley said. "I also wonder why she moved here."

Lisa hadn't been wondering about *that*. She was wondering what the new girl looked like. Lisa knew that a person's appearance shouldn't matter. It was what was inside that counted. But she was still curious.

A girl walked up to Lisa and Ashley. She was very pretty, with bright red cheeks and sparkly dark eyes and black hair falling all the way to her hips. "Are you girls in fourth grade?" she asked.

"Yes," Ashley said.

"You're both pretty," the girl said. "Are you popular?"

Lisa shrugged. "I guess."

"Why does that matter?" the rubber chicken asked from inside Lisa's backpack.

Lisa ignored him. The other girls couldn't hear him, because, as you should recall, only Lisa and Nate could hear Ed speak.

The girl stuck out her hand. "I'm Jennifer Morales. I'm new."

"I'm Ashley Chang," Ashley said as she shook her hand.

Lisa shook Jennifer's hand next. "And I'm Lisa Zupinski. I love the outfit you're wearing."

Ed whistled. "That getup looks like it cost big bucks."

Lisa had seen that outfit at the mall the

11

week before. It was pink silk, trimmed with sequins that said "Princess" on the butt. And it cost $257, which was $207 more than Lisa's mother had been willing to spend.

Jennifer looked down at her dress. "Oh, thanks," she said. "My mom bought me twelve new outfits last week. I was getting tired of my clothes."

"Are you going to be in Mrs. Crabpit's class?" Ashley asked.

Jennifer nodded. "Is Mrs. Crabpit pretty and popular?"

"That Jennifer sure is into being pretty and popular," Ed said.

"You'll love Mrs. Crabpit," Ashley told Jennifer. "If you're a fan of the Wicked Witch of the West, the Big Bad Wolf, and Voldemort."

The five-minute bell rang. A smelly woman approached them. **"Fun's over!"** she screamed. **"Move your butts into my classroom!"**

"Who was that ornery, odorous ogre?" Jennifer asked.

"Mrs. Crabpit," Lisa and Ashley said.

The three girls shivered. So did Ed, inside Lisa's backpack.

They headed to class along with everyone else, except for Dan the Dawdler, because he was a dawdler.

Mrs. Crabpit called Jennifer to the front of the classroom. "This is Jennifer Morales," she told the students.

Jennifer waved with one hand and held her nose with the other because of Mrs. Crabpit's bad smell.

"Does anyone have a question for Jennifer?" Mrs. Crabpit asked.

Lisa raised her hand. "Will you play with me and Ashley at recess?"

Jennifer looked her up and down. "I'll think about it and get back to you," she said.

Ed asked Jennifer why she was such a snob. But, of course, Jennifer couldn't hear him. (At this point in the book, you had better know why she couldn't hear the rubber chicken.)

Next, Nate asked Jennifer where she used to live.

"L.A.," she said. "Also known as the City of Angels. Everyone is beautiful there, and I chatted with TV stars almost every day."

Ashley asked which TV stars Jennifer had chatted with.

Jennifer said she used to go to school with a boy who was in a laundry detergent commercial. Also, the aunt of a girl in her old Brownie troop was on a reality TV show, but got voted off on the second day.

Jason Johnson stared at Jennifer through his glasses, and asked what a beautiful girl like her was doing in their town of Boring, Arizona.

Jennifer said she had moved because her parents were foolish and misguided, and also because her mother got a dumb job promotion.

Michelle Bell asked about Jennifer's position on global warming.

Jennifer wrinkled her eyebrows and said, "What's that?"

Dan the Dawdler entered the classroom and asked who she was.

Jennifer said, "I'm someone who's on time for school."

Then Mrs. Crabpit told Jennifer to sit down so that the class could resume their regular routine.

After Jennifer took her seat, Mrs. Crabpit yelled at everyone. That was their regular routine.

Finally, the bell rang for recess.

Lisa went to Jennifer's desk. "Did you make a decision yet?" she asked. "Do you want to play with my best friend Ashley and me during recess?"

"You'll find out in the next chapter," Jennifer said.

Okay, she didn't really say that. But ending the chapter here would add suspense to the book, don't you think?

The End.

Chapter 3
It's All Ed's Fault
(Sort Of)

Lisa stood at Jennifer's desk. Jennifer looked her up and down. Then she said, "I'll let you into my club."

"Club?" Lisa asked.

"Yes, I'm forming an exclusive club for pretty and popular girls. After a lot of thought, I decided to call it the Pretty and Popular Girls Club. You may be a member."

"Wow! Thanks," Lisa said. "Who else is

invited? There are a lot of nice girls here."

"Nice?" Jennifer pounded her fist on the desk. "What does *nice* have to do with anything? Do you hear the word *nice* anywhere in the Pretty and Popular Girls Club?"

Lisa shook her head.

"Plus, it's an exclusive club," Jennifer said. "The fewer girls we have, the more exclusive and better it'll be."

"Who else is in the club?" Lisa asked.

"Who was that girl I met before school?" Jennifer asked. "I'd like to invite her. She's pretty."

"And very—" Lisa clapped her hand over her mouth. She was going to say *nice*. She had forgotten that being nice wasn't important. "She's very popular," Lisa said. "Her name is Ashley Chang."

"Okay. I'll invite her. And we'll need one more girl." Jennifer walked out of the classroom.

Lisa followed her.

"You forgot about me!" Ed shouted from inside Lisa's backpack.

Hopefully, you remember that only Ed's owners could hear the rubber chicken. And if you don't remember who Ed's owners were, then there's little hope for you (Hint: Nate and Lisa Zupinski).

Sometimes Ed's owners wished they couldn't hear him. Today, for instance. Ed was screaming, **"Hey! Don't leave me in** this smelly classroom! Hurry up and get me out of here!" He could be very annoying.

Lisa covered her ears, rushed into the classroom, grabbed her backpack, and joined Jennifer outside.

Jennifer pointed at Brittany Billingsworth. "She's pretty," she muttered. "Is she popular?"

Lisa shrugged. "I guess."

"Then I guess we have our club," Jennifer said.

"If Ashley and Brittany even want to be in your club," the rubber chicken said.

"If Ashley and Brittany even want to be in your club," Lisa said.

Jennifer tossed her long, shiny hair and smiled. "Oh, they'll want to. Everyone wants to be in the Pretty and Popular Girls Club."

"I don't," Ed said.

"That's good," Lisa replied.

"Yes, it is a good club," Jennifer said. Then she asked Ashley and Brittany if they wanted to be in an exclusive club just for pretty and popular girls.

"What do we do in the club?" Ashley asked.

"We act pretty and popular," Jennifer told her.

"I'm in," Ashley said.

"And we exclude people."

"I'm in," Brittany said.

Jennifer smiled. "Perfect. Now let's make some rules. First, we need a club president."

Ashley raised her hand. "I—"

Jennifer cut her off. "Thank you for nominating me."

"But I didn't—"

Jennifer interrupted Ashley again. "I'd be honored to serve as your president."

"Shouldn't we vote on it?" Lisa asked.

"As club president," Jennifer said, "I get to decide how we choose our president." She put her chin on her hand as if she were deep in thought. "I've decided we won't vote on it."

"But—" Lisa started to say.

"Now for the rules," Jennifer said. "Rule

number one: everyone in the club must be pretty and popular. Rule number two—Yuck!"

"What kind of rule is *Yuck*?" Brittany asked.

Jennifer pointed to Lisa's open backpack. "You're carrying around a rubber chicken."

"Duh," Ed said.

"It's yucky," Jennifer said.

"Oh, yeah? Well, I think you're yucky!" Ed shouted.

"Lisa Zupinski, you're not in our club anymore," Jennifer said. "Your rubber chicken is too yucky."

"You wouldn't want to be in her club, anyway," Ed said.

Jennifer started to walk away. "Come on, Ash and Brit," she said.

"Call me Ashley," Ashley said.

"Call me Brittany," Brittany said.

"I'm club president," Jennifer said. "Rule number two is that your names are Ash and Brit. Now let's get away from that yucky rubber chicken."

Ashley and Brittany told Lisa they were sorry. Then they followed Jennifer.

"**You'll be sorry, all right!**" Ed called after them.

Lisa took Ed out of her backpack and clutched him to her chest.

"Sorry I ruined your chance to be in Jennifer's club," Ed told her.

"That's okay," Lisa said. "It's a dumb club, anyway." She used the Hawaiian lei around Ed's neck to wipe her wet eyes.

Chapter 4
The Worlds' Shortest Handball Game

Nate was showing Benny B. Benjamin how to make spitwads when Jennifer, Ashley, and Brittany walked over.

"What are you doing?" Ashley asked.

"Shh!" Jennifer said. "You can't talk to those boys. They're not in our club."

"Nate!" Ed shouted from the other side of the playground. **"Bean those girls with your spitwads! They**

were mean to your sister."

"Were you mean to Lisa?" Nate asked Jennifer.

She shrugged. "I only have to be nice to people in our club. That's rule number three."

"I should make sure Lisa is all right," Ashley said.

"Not now, Ash," Jennifer said. "There is urgent club business to discuss. We have to make a plan to get even more pretty and popular."

Nate rushed away to find Lisa. She was sitting next to Ed. Her eyes were red and she was sniffling. Nate hadn't seen Lisa looking that sad since her Peepee Patsy doll had stained her favorite dress.

"Lisa, what's wrong?" Nate asked her. "Why are you sitting all alone at recess?"

"All alone? What am I, chopped liver?" the supernatural rubber chicken asked. "Lisa isn't alone. I'm keeping her very good company, sharing my favorite songs with her. You know, I sing like a bird."

"A screech owl," Lisa muttered.

"Do you recognize this song?" Ed sang, "Somewhere over the rainbow, bluebirds fly," in a loud, squawky voice.

Lisa covered her ears. "I wish *you'd* fly over the rainbow and stay there," she told the rubber chicken.

Nate put his hand over Ed's beak to stop the wretched singing.

Lisa thanked her brother.

"Do you want to play handball with me?" Nate asked.

Because she was so grateful that Nate had stopped Ed's horrible singing, and because she had nothing else to do, she agreed to play handball.

As they walked over to the handball court, Nate kept his hand clamped over Ed's beak.

Nate put the rubber chicken on the side-line and told him, "If you promise not to sing, you can be the rubber chicken referee."

Ed sighed. "Okay, I promise. But you just don't appreciate a good voice when you hear it."

Nate served the ball.

Lisa hit it and walked away.

Nate followed her. "What's the matter?" he asked.

"I played handball, just like I said I would," Lisa told Nate. "Once I remembered how much I disliked it, I stopped."

"That's silly of you," Ed said.

"Oh, yeah?" Lisa yelled at Ed. "I'm never bringing you to school again."

"Now *that's* really silly of you," Ed said.

"You can go to school with me," Nate offered.

"In your disgusting backpack?" Ed asked. "That's even sillier."

"It's great," Nate said. "There's plenty of room for you. The snail and the beetle and the old chewing gum I added to my backpack this morning don't take up too much space."

"Gross," Lisa and Ed both said.

Nate shrugged. Then he crawled into some bushes to search for more insects to put into his backpack.

Chapter 5
The Chicken Takes a Lickin'

After school, Nate and Lisa walked into their house and said hello to their mother. She was at the computer as usual.

"How was your day?" she asked.

"Bad. Mrs. Crabpit smelled worse than ever," Nate said.

Ms. Zupinski turned around and smiled. "Everything will turn out great."

"I got kicked out of the Pretty and Popular

Girls Club today," Lisa said.

"You think that's bad," Ed said from inside Lisa's backpack. "Jennifer Morales called me yucky today, and you twins insulted my singing skills."

"What skills?" Nate asked. "You have no singing skills."

"Were you singing today?" Lisa asked the rubber chicken. "All I heard was shrieking."

"Everything will turn out great." Ms. Zupinski kept smiling at her computer.

Nate asked his mother what she was working on.

"It's a secret," she said. "Top secret. Secret with a capital *S*."

Nate shrugged. "No big deal. I was just

asking to be polite."

"All right. Since you want to know so badly, I'll tell you," Ms. Zupinski said. "I'm writing a children's book about the power of thinking good thoughts."

"Huh?" Nate asked.

"Show them, Plop." Ms. Zupinski pointed to the dog under her chair.

Plop wagged her tail.

"See?" Ms. Zupinski said. "Plop is thinking good thoughts."

"I still don't get it," Nate said.

"Suppose you're worried about your grades," his mother said.

Nate scratched his head. "Why would I worry about my grades? I have much more important things to think about. Like handball."

"That's why you have a D average," Ed pointed out.

"So, Nate, you're worried about your grades," his mother said.

Nate shook his head. "I just told you—"

She interrupted him. "You only need to *think* that you'll get straight As, and then you'll get them."

"What about doing homework and studying?" Lisa asked.

Ms. Zupinski scowled. "You shouldn't try those crazy schemes. They'll get in the way of thinking positive thoughts." She stared at the computer again.

"How far are you on your book?" Nate asked his mother.

"I'm almost done," she said. "I've thought about writing it, thought about my book getting published with a snazzy cover, and thought about it becoming a best seller."

"Where is it?" Lisa asked.

Ms. Zupinski pointed to her head. "Up here. I haven't bothered with the pesky details of actually writing anything, but my thoughts about this book are very positive."

"How do all those positive thoughts manage to fit into your mother's tiny brain?" Ed asked.

Nate and Lisa slowly backed out of the room.

Plop followed them. She climbed on Lisa's legs and sniffed.

"Oh, how sweet." Lisa patted the dog's head. "I think Plop wants to say hello to Ed."

"That's okay. Really," Ed said.

"Eddie, say hello to your pal Ploppy." Lisa took the rubber chicken out of her backpack and kneeled down with him in her arms.

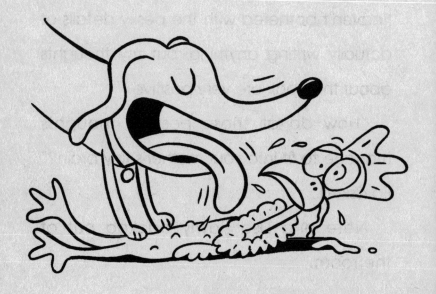

"No-o-o!" Ed yelled.

But it was too late.

Plop was already licking Ed all over.

"Hey!" Ms. Zupinski called from the bathroom. "There's barely any water in the toilet. Plop must have been drinking out of it again."

"Yuck! Blecch! Phooey!" Ed yelled as Plop kept licking him.

"Don't worry, Eddie," Lisa said. "I'll give you a bath."

"No-o-o!" Ed hated baths even more than he hated being licked by Plop.

But Lisa loved giving baths more than anything.

She carried the rubber chicken into

the bathroom and said, "I'm having very good thoughts about getting you nice and clean."

Chapter 6
Bubble Trouble

Lisa started filling the bathtub with water.

"Agh!" Ed cried. "Not **another bath!**"

Lisa poured bath bubbles into the tub. "I haven't given you a bath in a long time."

"You just gave me one yesterday," Ed reminded her.

"I know," Lisa told him. "Like I said, it's been a long time. And today I want to get you extra soapy, with tons of fun bubbles."

"Bubbles are not fun." Ed sighed. "I hate baths."

"You'll learn to love them," Lisa said.

"I've been around for hundreds of years," the rubber chicken told Lisa. "I have never loved baths, nor even liked baths. I will not learn to love them."

"Remember my mother's advice: think positive thoughts." Lisa smiled at Ed.

"Okay. I'm positive that I don't want a bath," the rubber chicken said.

Lisa put him into the tub and covered him with bubbles. "Oh, you look so darling!" she exclaimed.

"Please don't call me darling," the rubber

chicken told her. "I'm dashing and hand-
some, *not* darling."

"If you say so, Eddie Wetty." Lisa dabbed
soap on his cheeks. "Not only will you look
great, you'll smell great too. Like a garden full
of lilacs, according to the label on this lovely
soap."

Ed groaned.

"I'm going to bring you to school and
show you off to Jennifer," Lisa said.

He frowned. "I don't like Jennifer. She
called me ugly, and she was mean to
you."

"That will change once you give her a
superpower," Lisa said as she scrubbed the
sides of the rubber chicken's face.

"Hey! You got soap in my ears!" the rubber chicken yelled.

"Silly chicken." Lisa laughed. "You don't even have ears."

"What? I can't hear you," Ed said. "The soap is blocking my ears."

"You don't have ears!" Lisa said.

"What?" Ed repeated. "The tiny ears hidden on the sides of my face are now full of bubbles. I can't hear anything. Did you say something?"

"I wish that you'll make the next person who touches you super gracious."

"Get that stupid lilac soap

out of my ears first!" the rubber chicken demanded.

But Lisa wasn't paying attention. She was imagining what would happen once Jennifer became super gracious.

Gracious people are kind and polite. Once Jennifer is super gracious, she will be nice to people. She'll let anyone join her club, Lisa thought, *even people who carry around ugly rubber—*

"I'm deaf now!" the rubber chicken yelled. **"I hope you're happy with yourself, girlie. You blocked up my ears and made me deaf!"**

Lisa lifted him by his feet and shook him hard from side to side.

"Agh!" Ed screamed. **"What in the world are you doing?"**

"Clearing your ears," Lisa told him. "Duh."

"Well, at least I can hear again," Ed said.

"Aren't you going to thank me?" Lisa asked.

"For what? Making me smell like a lilac

garden? Trying to destroy my hearing? Shaking me so hard I now have a headache the size of Cleveland?"

"Take it easy." Lisa poured a bucket of cold water over the rubber chicken to rinse him off. "We have a big day ahead of us tomorrow. You'll need all your energy to give Jennifer a superpower."

"You've taken all my energy. I have nothing left to give," Ed said. "And I didn't even hear your wish very well."

Lisa didn't pay attention to him. She was imagining what Jennifer would be like once she was super gracious.

Jennifer will probably insist that I play with her, Lisa thought.

"You wanted Jennifer to be super what?" the rubber chicken asked.

Lisa didn't answer him. She was busy trying to think good thoughts.

Jennifer may even say she's sorry for being mean to me today, Lisa thought.

She couldn't wait to make Jennifer super gracious.

Chapter 7

Fear of Flying

The next morning, Lisa, Nate, and the rubber chicken sat at the kitchen table.

"Ed is going to give that new girl, Jennifer, a superpower today," Lisa told Nate. She nibbled on sliced strawberries.

"Thaz gray," Nate said as he chewed his ham-sausage-bacon-steak omelet.

"Do you mean 'That's great'?" Lisa asked her brother.

"Yeh," Nate said with his mouth full. "I seh, 'Thaz gray.' "

"Once Jennifer gets her superpower, she won't be so mean to Ed and me," Lisa said. "Gracious people don't keep someone out of their club just because they think her rubber chicken is gross."

"If she thinks Ed is gross, how are you going to get her to touch him?" Nate asked.

"Ed looks a lot better today. I gave him a bath." Lisa pinched Ed's cheek.

"He's still an uhly rurrer chih," Nate said as he finished his meat omelet.

"A what?" Lisa asked.

An ugly rubber chicken! Nate shouted.

"I'm rubber and I'm a chicken," Ed said,

"but I'm not ugly. Hmph!"

Nate rolled his eyes. "Okay, you're gorgeous. Whatever you say. But for some reason, Jennifer thinks you're ugly. She won't want to touch you."

"I'll make Ed look really cute," Lisa said. "I'll dress him up in doll clothes. In fact, Ed and Peepee Patsy are about the same size. She has an adorable pink-striped dress he could wear."

"No way!" Ed exclaimed. "I will not wear a doll's dress, especially a doll who goes peepee. There are yellow spots on her dress. And you know what that means."

"Eww," Lisa said.

"I got it." Nate snapped his fingers. "Instead

of asking Jennifer to go to the chicken, we'll bring the chicken to her."

"Huh?" Lisa said.

"We'll throw Ed at Jennifer," Nate said. "Once the supernatural rubber chicken lands on her, the spell should work."

"What if I don't land on her?" Ed asked. "What if I land on my face on hard cement?"

"Are you doubting my throwing ability?" Nate said.

"Sure am," Ed said. "My head could crack open."

"Oh, you're such a worrywart," Nate told him. "You're made of rubber. Rubber doesn't crack. If you landed on hard cement, you'd probably just bounce around."

"That makes me feel better," Ed said.

"Of course, your brain would get all smooshed," Nate added. "So you probably would never have another thought again."

"The plan is on," Lisa said. "I can't wait to bring Ed to school."

"I can't wait to throw him at Jennifer," Nate said.

"I can't wait to find a good lawyer and take you to court," the rubber chicken said.

Chapter 8
Tossed Chicken with a Side of Cockroach

"This is it," Lisa told Nate as they got off the school bus the next morning. "In a few minutes, you'll hurl our rubber chicken at Jennifer. And if everything goes according to plan, she'll become super gracious."

"What?" Ed shouted from inside Nate's backpack. **"It's hard to hear you inside this backpack. Agh! I feel something crawling on my butt."**

Nate shrugged. "Don't worry about it. It's probably just the cockroach I found yesterday."

"Get me out of here!" Ed screamed.

Lisa pointed at the playground. "There's Jennifer."

"Time to get Ed out of here," Nate said.

He took the rubber chicken out of his backpack. "Looks like you've made a friend, Ed. There's a cockroach on your butt."

"Eww." Lisa wrinkled her nose.

"What should we name this cute little fellow?" Nate asked.

"How about calling him Go Away," Ed said.

Nate picked up the cockroach. "Don't listen to Ed," he told the bug. "He's just nervous about my chicken-tossing abilities." Nate returned the cockroach to his backpack.

"I *should* be nervous," Ed said. "I'll either land on a girl who thinks I'm disgusting or land on the hard ground. I don't know what's worse."

"Landing on the hard ground probably would be worse," Nate said. "Although, after you land on Jennifer, she'll probably throw you onto the hard ground."

"Great. Just great," Ed said.

"Wait!" Lisa said. "I'll try asking Jennifer to touch you."

She grabbed the rubber chicken and walked over to Jennifer.

Jennifer was kissing a mirror that she was holding in her long red fingernails.

"I gave my rubber chicken a bath," Lisa said. "Don't you think he's cute now?"

"No, I don't," Jennifer said. "No matter how clean he looks, he'll always be ugly."

"No matter how pretty Jennifer looks, she'll always be a jerk," Ed said.

Lisa tried again. "My rubber chicken is really soft." She held out the rubber chicken. "Feel him."

"Yuck! No way!" Jennifer yelled.

Lisa sighed. "So much for that idea."

"Time to play a little game of catch," Nate said.

"No-o-o!" Ed screamed, as Nate took him from Lisa's hands.

"Agh!" Ed screamed, as Nate hurled him at Jennifer.

"I'm getting dizzy!" Ed yelled as he flew through the air.

"How could you risk my life

like this?" Ed asked as he got near Jennifer.

Nate shrugged. "It wasn't that difficult."

"Ow!" Ed exclaimed as he landed on Jennifer's face.

"Ow!" Jennifer exclaimed as Ed landed on her face. **"Something just landed on my face!"**

She grabbed Ed by his feet. "Yuck! It's that disgusting rubber chicken."

"Did someone just call me disgusting?" Ed asked. "I'm still very dizzy."

Nate and Lisa smiled at each other. "We did it!" Lisa said.

"Thanks to my great throwing arm," Nate said.

"Hey, Jennifer, are you feeling gracious, by any chance?" Lisa asked her.

"No!" Jennifer screamed. **"Take back your ugly rubber chicken, you stupid weirdo."** She threw Ed back to Nate.

"Agh!" Ed yelled again.

Jennifer put her hands on her hips. "Lisa Zupinski, you will never be in my Pretty and Popular Girls Club! Never, ever, ever, ever, ever!"

Lisa hung her head. "I guess you're not feeling very gracious."

"No way," Jennifer said.

"But you touched my rubber chicken," Lisa said.

"Yeah," Jennifer said. "It was totally gross."

"For your information, I didn't like touching you either," Ed told her.

Lisa frowned. "Ed, shouldn't the super-power be working by now?"

"Superpower?" Ed asked. "What? I feel dizzy."

Lisa realized there was a problem.

Nate realized there was a problem.

"Let's call Dave," they both said.

Chapter 9
Dave to the Rescue!

Nate and Lisa left Ed on the playground so he wouldn't hear them talking about him. Then they walked to the school payphone to call Dave for help.

Dave was their older brother. He used to own the supernatural rubber chicken. But he gave Ed to the twins when he left home to surf the waves in Malibu, California.

So who owns the rubber chicken now?

Nate and Lisa, of course.

Duh.

Nate called Dave while Lisa stood next to him.

Luckily, Dave answered right away. "Hey, dude," he said.

"I'm glad I reached you," Nate said.

"What's wrong?" Dave asked. "Are you sick? Injured? Do you have another weird pimple on your butt?"

"You promised not to mention the weird pimple on my butt," Nate said.

"You have a weird pimple on your butt?" Lisa asked.

"So what's wrong, Nate?" Dave asked.

"It's Ed," Nate told him.

"Oh, hi, Ed," Dave said. "Your voice sounds like my brother Nate's."

"No, this is Nate," Nate said.

"Dude, why did you pretend to be Ed?" Dave asked.

"I didn't," Nate told his brother. "When I said 'It's Ed,' I was trying to tell you something's happened to Ed."

"Not Ed!" Dave started sobbing. "Not my poor, sweet, little rubber chicken dude! He's only 438 years old, give or take a few years— way too young to die." He cried some more.

"It's not that bad," Nate said.

"Not that bad?" Dave asked. **"Have you no feelings? No heart?"** he screamed. "My favorite rubber chicken in the whole wide world is dead, and you tell me it's not that bad." Dave blew his nose. "Well, at least he's in chicken heaven. Maybe he'll meet up with his Grandma Edwina there."

"Ed's alive," Nate said.

"Oh, phew." Dave breathed a sigh of relief. "Why didn't you tell me?"

"But we think he's very sick."

"Oh, no!" Dave took a sharp breath. "Why didn't you tell me?"

"He may have lost his superpowers," Nate said.

"Oh, yikes!" Dave gasped. "Why didn't you tell me?"

"I'm telling you now."

"Oh, right." Dave breathed another sigh of relief. Then he said, "Hey, wait a minute. He never lost his superpowers when I owned him. What did you do to him, dude?"

"We didn't do anything to him," Nate said. "Lisa told Ed to make the first person who touched him super gracious. And this mean girl, Jennifer, touched him. But she's still really mean."

"Whoa, sounds like the rubber chicken dude lost his superpowers."

"I know!" Nate said. "What should we do?"

"Dude, I have the perfect solution," Dave said.

"I'm so glad I called you."

"Tell Jennifer the waves are really awesome here in Malibu," Dave said.

Nate raised his eyebrows. "Huh?"

"Once Jennifer moves to Malibu to surf, you won't have to worry about her."

"But—" Nate said.

"I'm glad I could help you," Dave said.

"But—" Nate said.

"I have to go catch some waves."

"But—" Nate said.

"Hang ten." Dave clicked off his phone.

Chapter 10
Grace What?

Nate and Lisa walked back to Jennifer. Nate asked her whether she liked to surf.

"Shut your pie hole," she told him.

Nate sighed. "I guess you're not feeling very gracious today."

"Does this answer your question?" Jennifer screamed. She made a fist and tried to punch him in the face.

Luckily (for Nate, anyway), just as Jennifer's

fist was closing in on Nate's nose, she fell side-
ways and landed fist-first on the blacktop of
the playground.

Nate stood over her. "Now are you feeling
gracious?" he asked.

"No!" she yelled. **"I'm feeling mad
that I didn't get to punch you! I'm
going to try again."** She stood up and
made a fist.

She accidentally punched herself in the face.

Then she fell over again.

Nate and Lisa picked up Ed and walked away.

"Why didn't you make Jennifer super gracious?" Nate asked the rubber chicken.

"Super gracious?" Ed asked. "You wanted me to make Jennifer gracious?"

"Duh," Lisa said. "Remember when I gave you a bath, I told you to make Jennifer super gracious? I wanted her to be super nice to people."

"I remember that you got soap in my ears and I could hardly hear anything."

"Uh-oh." Nate frowned. "What did you

think Lisa told you to do?"

"I thought you wanted me to make Jennifer super *graceless*," the rubber chicken said.

"Graceless." Lisa's eyebrows crinkled as she thought about it. "That means without grace."

"Clumsy," Nate said.

"Klutzy," Ed said.

"I'm going to get you, Nate Lupinski!" Jennifer called out. She ran toward him, but tripped and fell on her face.

"Graceless," Nate, Ed, and Lisa said together.

Chapter 11

Have a Nice Trip.
See You in the Fall.

Jennifer stood up and brushed stray pebbles off her face.

"Are you okay?" Ashley asked her.

"Of course I'm okay." Jennifer flicked an ant off the tip of her nose. "I fell on purpose."

"You did?" Brittany's mouth dropped open.

Jennifer nodded. "As president of the Pretty and Popular Girls Club, I hereby declare rule number four: We're all supposed to act really clumsy."

Brittany fell down. "Clumsy like this?" she asked as she lay on the playground.

"Perfect." Jennifer smiled. Then she pushed Ashley on top of Brittany.

The bell rang. Mrs. Crabpit rushed over and screamed, **"Stop fooling around and get up! School's starting. Move it, move it, move it!"**

Ashley and Brittany stood up and dusted themselves off.

All the students started walking to their classrooms.

Jennifer smoothed her hair. Her elbow accidentally bumped Hulk Paine's chest, causing them both to fall over.

They fell onto Lisa, Nate, and Ed.

Lisa, Nate, and Ed fell onto Mrs. Crabpit.

As Mrs. Crabpit lay sprawled on the black-top, she shouted, **"Nate and Lisa Zupinski! How dare you knock me over?"**

Before the twins could say they were sorry, Mrs. Crabpit ordered them to stay in the class-room during recess and lunch.

"Don't worry," Ed told them. "Sometimes things don't seem to be working out, but they really do in the end."

"Oh, be quiet," Nate and Lisa said.

"How dare you tell me to be quiet!" Mrs. Crabpit screamed. "Not only will you be in my classroom for recess and lunch, but you'll stay there for two hours after school too."

"Yes, Mrs. Crabpit," the twins said. They glared at Ed and said, "Thanks a lot."

"You're welcome," Mrs. Crabpit said.

Nate stuffed Ed into his backpack headfirst.

Chapter 12

A Klutz Can Drive
You Nuts

"I sure am good at this superpower stuff," Ed said. "Lisa wanted Jennifer to be graceless, and she got just what she wished for."

"Gracious! Not graceless!" Nate exclaimed.

"Well, why didn't she say so?" Ed asked.

Jennifer walked into the classroom, tripped over her feet, and fell on the floor.

So Ashley and Brittany tripped over *their*

feet and fell on the floor.

"Sit down and stop fooling around!" Mrs. Crabpit yelled.

Jennifer tried to sit down, but tripped on her chair and landed on her bottom.

Ashley and Brittany fell down on purpose and landed on their bottoms too.

"You three girls will stay inside for recess and lunch with Nate and Lisa," Mrs. Crabpit said.

Nate and Lisa were glad to see the Pretty and Popular Girls get in trouble. Nate took Ed out of his backpack so he could see the girls' huge frowns.

Mrs. Crabpit told the class to get out their grammar books and pencils. "For the next hour and a half," she said, "I will be talking all about the history of the comma. I think you'll find it fascinating."

Nate thought he'd fall asleep.

Lisa thought she'd rather be shopping for clothes or playing with her stuffed animals or even watching grass grow.

Ed thought he wanted bubble bath in his ears again, so he wouldn't have to listen to Mrs. Crabpit.

Jennifer dropped her grammar book and pencil onto the floor.

Ashley and Brittany dropped their books and pencils onto the floor too.

Mrs. Crabpit was so frustrated with the Pretty and Popular Girls that she threw her arms up in the air. This made her odor stronger than ever. A swirl of stink wafted out the window.

A nearby mole was so disturbed by Mrs. Crabpit's odor that he dug a hole deep in the ground and rushed through it. The mole didn't stop digging and running until he reached China. He popped out of the hole, hoping  to relax with some chow mein and black tea. But the odor still clung to the mole.

So the mole dug more holes, traveling the world in an attempt to get rid of the nasty smell. The stink finally left the mole twenty years later in the Arabian Desert. The mole was so excited to be odor-free that he died. Luckily, he had already dug a deep hole to be buried in.

But where were we?

Ah, yes. Back in the classroom, Mrs. Crabpit ordered the Pretty and Popular Girls to stay after school along with Nate and Lisa.

Ed screeched out a highly annoying victory song, until Lisa shut his beak with a rubber band and put him into her backpack.

Then Mrs. Crabpit ordered Jennifer, Ashley, and Brittany to pick up the pencils and books they had dropped.

The Pretty and Popular Girls picked up

their pencils and grammar books. Then they dropped them again.

"**Yoʉ're driving me crazy!**" Mrs. Crabpit yelled.

"Sorry," Jennifer said. She fell out of her chair.

Ashley and Brittany told the teacher they were sorry too. Then they fell out of their chairs.

Mrs. Crabpit thought about leaving her teaching job and doing something less stressful—for instance, becoming a firefighter or trapeze artist. But she knew the children would be miserable without her. So she decided to keep teaching.

She spent the next hour and a half lecturing the class about the history of the comma. Then she spent forty-five minutes talking about the history of the apostrophe.

Her students all took long naps.

Except for Dan the Dawdler. He was still walking to school, picking up and examining every leaf he saw on the way. He saw thousands of leaves on the way.

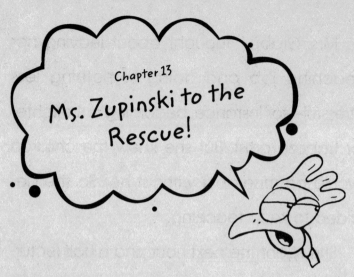

Chapter 13
Ms. Zupinski to the Rescue!

Jennifer, Brittany, and Ashley spent their after-school detention hard at work. They ranked their classmates from prettiest to ugliest and from most popular to least popular. They also fell out of their chairs a lot.

Nate spent detention playing with the insects in his backpack.

Lisa wrote long letters complaining about Mrs. Crabpit. She addressed them to the principal, the school board, the governor, and her favorite boy band, The Smiling Hacks. She also sent The Smiling Hacks a nice drawing of hearts and flowers, and asked them for an autographed photo or a T-shirt worn by Scam, their lead singer.

Finally, once the two-hour detention was over, Mrs. Crabpit told everyone to get out of her classroom.

Jennifer tripped in the doorway as she tried to leave.

Brittany and Ashley tripped over Jennifer.

Then they all helped one another off the floor.

"I guess we missed the school bus," Nate said.

"My mother will drive us home," Jennifer said.

"Oh, great!" Lisa exclaimed.

"*Us*, meaning Ash, Brit, and me," Jennifer said. "Only Pretty and Popular Girls are allowed to ride in my car."

The three girls walked out, tripping again on the way to the parking lot.

Lisa, Nate, and Ed headed to the payphone.

Nate called their mother and told her that they had to stay after school. "We missed our bus," he said. "Can we have a ride home?"

"Say please, Nate," Lisa whispered.

So Nate whispered, "Please, Nate," into the phone.

86

"I can help you with a ride home," Ms. Zupinski said.

"Great!" Nate said.

"Say thank you, Nate," Lisa whispered.

"Thank you, Nate," he whispered into the phone. "Should we wait for you in front of school?" he asked his mother.

"Huh?" she said. "I meant that I can help you with a ride home by telling you to think positively. If you think that you'll find a way home, then it will happen. Just make sure you throw good, strong thoughts into the air."

"That's all the help you're giving us?" Nate complained.

"Of course not. I'll also think positive thoughts for you."

"How about getting into your car and driving to the school and picking us up?" Nate asked.

"Keep thinking those strong thoughts," Ms. Zupinski said.

"Mom, we need a ride," Nate told her.

"Yes. I'm sure you'll get one," Ms. Zupinski said. "Eventually, anyway. You might not get that ride today or tomorrow, but it will come if your thoughts are strong enough."

"Thanks." Nate hung up the phone.

"Is Mom going to pick us up?" Lisa asked her brother.

Nate shook his head.

"Do you really have a weird pimple on your butt?" Lisa asked.

Nate nodded.

The twins walked home.

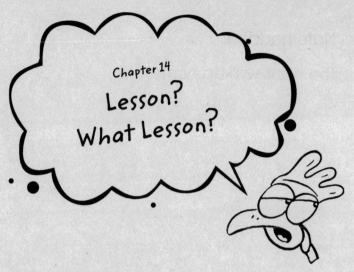

Chapter 14
Lesson?
What Lesson?

Nate and Lisa came to school the next morning with Ed inside Nate's backpack.

"Jennifer might not be super graceless anymore," Ed said. "The superpowers only last a day or two."

"Even one day of being super graceless might have taught Jennifer a lesson," Lisa said.

"Not to wear high heels to school?" Nate asked.

Lisa shook her head. "Hopefully, she's realized that nobody's perfect, and that it's wrong to exclude people."

Lisa pointed at Jennifer, who was sitting on a bench with Ashley and Brittany. "I'll find out if she learned her lesson."

Lisa went over to the Pretty and Popular Girls, sat next to Jennifer, and said hi.

Jennifer poured water from her water bottle onto Lisa's pink sneakers. "Oops."

"Aren't you going to say you're sorry?" Lisa asked.

Jennifer smiled. "Nope."

Brittany fell against Ashley. "Oops."

Ashley fell against Brittany. "Oops."

"Why are you doing that?" Lisa asked.

"It's what Pretty and Popular Girls are supposed to do," Jennifer said.

"I don't think flailing around like an idiot looks very pretty," Lisa said. "And if you only have two friends, I wouldn't call you popular."

Mrs. Crabpit came up to them. "You girls had better behave today," she said.

"We will. Don't worry." Jennifer sipped water from her bottle.

After Mrs. Crabpit left, Lisa said, "You didn't spill your drink."

"Of course not. I don't want Mrs. Crabpit to give me detention again," Jennifer said. "I spilled water on you on purpose, Lisa. You'd better leave before I do it again."

Lisa walked away.

She found Nate and Ed by the hand-ball court. "Are the girls being nice now?" Nate asked.

"Yes," Lisa said. "If you think spilling water on someone is nice."

"I'd say no," Nate said.

"Jennifer isn't super graceless anymore. Now she's just pretending to be graceless." Lisa sighed. "I wish she'd be more caring about other people's feelings."

"Super caring?" Ed asked.

"Yes!" Lisa grinned. "Super caring! Great idea! I wish that the first person who touches our supernatural rubber chicken will become super caring," Lisa said. "And I sure hope that

Jennifer is the one who touches Ed first."

Nate moved his arm in circles. "I'm warming up my throwing arm. I'll be aiming the rubber chicken right at Jennifer again."

"Oh, no." Ed groaned. "Why did I suggest making Jennifer super caring?"

"Because you're a super caring, sweet little rubber chickie, Eddie."

Lisa tickled his chin.

Ed rolled his eyes.

Chapter 15
Who Cares?

Jennifer walked toward Mrs. Crabpit's classroom. Ashley and Brittany trailed her. Jennifer pretended to trip, landing daintily a few feet from the classroom door. Ashley and Brittany faked their own falls behind her.

While Jennifer was down, Nate flung the rubber chicken at her.

"Ack!" she screamed as Ed landed on her face again. "Get that yucky thing off me!"

Nate quickly scooped up the rubber chicken.

"I'm the one who should be upset," Ed said. "Some of Jennifer's lip gloss came off on me. I bet I now have a red, sticky, strawberry-scented butt."

Nate inspected the rubber chicken's bottom. Ed was right. His butt had bright red lip marks on it. Nate tried not to laugh.

"What are you so happy about?" Jennifer asked with a snarl.

"Uh, nothing," Nate said. "I'm, uh, just happy to see a pretty and popular girl like you."

"Do you really think I'm pretty and popular?" Jennifer asked.

Nate shrugged. "Sure."

"The prettiest and most popular girl in school?"

Nate thought Jennifer was the most annoying girl in school. He glanced at his wrist and said, "Look at the time!"

"How can you look at the time?" Jennifer

asked him. "You're not wearing a watch."

"Oh. Um. Uh." Nate tried to think of a good fib. "When I looked at my wrist, I saw that I had goose bumps. That must mean school is starting soon."

"You're weird," Jennifer told him.

"Gotta go!" Nate rushed inside the classroom and sat at his desk. He put Ed on his lap and whispered, "Thanks for making Jennifer super caring. I hope the spell works."

Everyone sat down right before the bell rang. Except for Dan the Dawdler. He was in the bathroom washing his hands, staring at himself in the mirror, and counting the hairs on his head.

"Get out your notebooks," Mrs. Crabpit

told the class. "Today, you will write a ten-page essay about your favorite insect."

Nate raised his

hand. "I have so many favorite insects— earwigs, tiger beetles, giant phasmids, the damsel-fly. How can I choose one favorite?"

"Pick one!" Mrs. Crabpit screamed. **"Any more questions?"**

Jennifer raised her hand. "Do you think I'm pretty and popular?"

"No," the teacher said.

"Are you saying that because you're really jealous?" Jennifer asked.

"No," the teacher said.

Jennifer raised her hand again. "Do you think the earrings I'm wearing match the style of my dress?" she asked.

"Stop asking questions and write the insect essay!" Mrs. Crabpit screamed.

"But I can't think about schoolwork during a time of crisis," Jennifer said.

"What crisis?" the teacher asked.

"The crisis of possibly wearing the wrong size earrings, of course!" Jennifer cried.

Mrs. Crabpit rolled her eyes. **"Get to work."**

"Do you think plaid is a good color for me?" Jennifer asked.

"I don't care!" Mrs. Crabpit screamed.

"I care," Jennifer said. "I care a lot about my looks. In fact, suddenly I care a lot about everything."

Nate gasped.

Lisa gasped.

Ed said, "Whoops."

Nate whispered to Ed on his lap, "You made Jennifer super caring. But she's not super sweet and nice like she's supposed to be. She just cares about herself even more than she used to."

"No whispering!" Mrs. Crabpit yelled. "I'm getting fed up with this class!"

"But not so fed up that you'd make us stay after school again, right?" Jennifer asked. "I care a lot about that too."

"Great idea, Jennifer," Mrs. Crabpit said. "The whole class will stay two hours after school. Any other questions?"

"Yes," Jennifer said. "Do you like the way I parted my hair today? Or should I wear the part a half-inch more to the left?"

Nate and Lisa plopped their heads on their desks.

"Should I try a zigzag part?" Jennifer asked. "Highlights? Should I go blonde?"

The rest of the students plopped their heads on their desks.

"Do you think I should wear a wig?"

Nobody answered except the rubber chicken, who muttered, "Sorry, but your big mouth can't hide your tiny brain." Then he plopped his head on Nate's desk.

"Tell me what to do with my hair!" Jennifer pleaded. "I really care what you think! Really, really, really!"

Mrs. Crabpit plopped her head on her desk too.

Chapter 16

Best Friends Forever. Well, Friendly Acquaintances, Anyway.

When the bell rang for recess, Jennifer headed toward the classroom door. Then she stopped at the doorway and turned around. "Brit and Ash," she said, "aren't you going to follow me?"

They both shook their heads.

"Why not?" Jennifer asked.

"You got the whole class in trouble today," Ashley said.

"Yeah," Brittany said. "Now we have to stay after school again."

Lisa stood in the doorway behind Jennifer. "Pardon me, please," she said. "I'd like to get by."

Hulk Paine rushed in front of Lisa, shoved Jennifer aside, and yelled, "Move it!"

Jennifer fell to the floor.

Brittany and Ashley stepped over her and walked away.

"What about our Pretty and Popular Girls Club?" Jennifer called after them. "Am I the only one who cares about it?"

"Yes," Brittany said. "We quit."

"And we're sorry for being mean to you before, Lisa," Ashley said.

Jennifer stayed on the floor and put her head in her hands. "How could they quit the club I care so much about?" she muttered.

Lisa and Nate helped Jennifer get up. "There are more important things in life to care about," Lisa said. "Being pretty and popular and in an exclusive club aren't the only things."

"I know that," Jennifer said. "I care about other things too. I care about trendy hats and expensive shoes and my teeth."

"Your teeth?" Nate asked.

"Yes," Jennifer said. "I spend a lot of time looking in the mirror and practicing my fake smiles. I like my teeth to be white and shiny." She smiled with her mouth open about an

inch. "I call this smile the Hollywood Happy Face."

Next, Jennifer closed her mouth and smiled. "I call this one the New Yorker."

Then, Jennifer smiled with the tip of her tongue over the edge of her teeth. "Here's my Supermodel Special."

"I don't like any of those fake smiles," Nate said.

Jennifer frowned. "That's too bad, because I care deeply about my smile."

"Why don't you just smile when something makes you happy instead of when you're trying to impress people?" Lisa asked.

"Wow! Smiling when I'm actually happy. Brilliant idea! I never thought of that,"

Jennifer said. "You seem really smart, Lisa. So I'd like to ask you about something that I care deeply about."

"World peace?" Lisa asked.

Jennifer shook her head. "Nah."

"Starving children in Africa?" Nate asked.

"Wrong. This involves something *really important*."

"Endangered species?" Lisa asked.

Jennifer shook her head again. "I really need to know whether I'm pretty and popular. Do you think I am?" she asked.

Lisa rolled her eyes. "I guess."

"Now that Brit and Ash have quit my Pretty and Popular Girls Club, will anyone be my friend?" Jennifer asked. "That's another thing I care a lot about."

"I'll be your friend," Lisa offered.

"Me too," Nate said. "Especially if you'll play handball with me."

Jennifer smiled.

"That's a genuine smile, isn't it?" Nate asked her.

"Sure is," Jennifer said.

"It's the best smile you have." Lisa smiled back.

Dan the Dawdler came out of the bathroom and walked over to them. "I was counting the hairs on my head, but had to stop at 13,497 because I didn't want to be late for school," he said.

"School started hours ago," Nate told him.

"It's already recess time."

"Oh." Dan shrugged. "Well, I guess I have a few more minutes to count hairs," he said. "Now where was I? 14,947? Or was that 14,379?" He shook his head. "I don't remember. I had better start over." He returned to the boys bathroom, counting. "One, two, three hairs. Four, five, six hairs. Seven, eight..."

After Dan the Dawdler left, Jennifer turned to Lisa and asked, "Why do you want to be my friend, Lisa? I was mean to you."

"I want to be your friend because I think it's mean to exclude people," Lisa said.

Nate called out, "And rubber chickens!" He tossed Ed to Lisa.

Lisa caught Ed and gave him a hug.

"Everyone deserves to be treated nicely," she said. "Even rubber chickens."

Jennifer nodded. "I guess you're right. Even ugly rubber chickens might have some good qualities."

"Who are you calling ugly?" Ed said.

"So have you realized now that everyone has good qualities?" Lisa asked Jennifer.

"I think so," she said. "For instance, Dan the Dawdler has really thick hair. Over 13,479 strands."

"I thought he counted 13,497 strands," Nate said.

Jennifer shrugged. "Whatever it is, it's a lot."

"If you had refused to talk to him because he wasn't in your club, you would never have known that about him," Lisa said.

"That's true," Jennifer said. "I guess from now on I shouldn't exclude people."

"Or rubber chickens," Ed said.

"Or rubber chickens?" Lisa asked Jennifer.

"Well, let's not get carried away," Jennifer replied.

"You want to play hopscotch?" Lisa asked her.

Jennifer smiled. "That would be great. You're a fun friend." Then she shouted, "Who wants to play hopscotch? Everyone's welcome!"

"I told you sometimes things don't seem to work out," Ed said, "but they really do in the end."

Lisa kissed him on the cheek. "You were right. And I know a great way to celebrate," she whispered to the rubber chicken. "As soon as we get home from school, I'll give you a lovely, soapy bubble bath."

"Agh!" Ed cried. "Not **another bath!**"

Don't be chicken!
Read the whole series!

"What's wrong with being a chicken?"

Fowl Language
June 2008

Fine Feathered Four Eyes
June 2008

Poultry in Motion
September 2008

For more information visit:
Supernaturalrubberchicken.com

How do you hatch a dragon egg?
Do dragon riders need reins?
How do you say *fly* in Draconic?
Find out everything you wanted to know
(and more!)

A PRACTICAL GUIDE TO
DRAGON RIDING

The follow-up to *The New York Times*
best-selling *A Practical Guide to Dragons*

How do you make a magic wand?
Why does a wizard wear robes? What goes
in to a potion of invisibility? Arch Mage
Lowadar invites you to join his school for
talented young wizards and explore the
magical world of wizardry.

A PRACTICAL GUIDE TO
WIZARDRY

FOR AGES SIX AND UP

It's truth or dare with a mystical twist!

"Fun and rollicking..."
-Young Adult Books Central

Nova and the Charmed Three
Can Nova rock her way past Ivy and into Joe's heart?

Yumi Talks the Talk
Nova's best friend Yumi gets a big surprise!

Carmen's Crystal Ball
Carmen Bernstein, pet psychic, is open for business.

Bella Goes Hollywood
Bella's on the case of a Hollywood prankster.

Maya Made Over
Maya decides it's time to remake her image.

Rani and the Wedding Ghost
Can Rani exorcise the wedding ghost?

TIME SPIES

"What a fun adventure! And a fascinating journey through history at the same time."
—Marion Dane Bauer,
author of the *Newbery Honor book*,
On My Honor

Strike it rich with Jack London in
Gold in the Hills
A Tale of the Klondike Gold Rush
March 2008

Solve a mystery on Mount Rushmore in
Message in the Mountain
A Tale of Mount Rushmore
May 2008

Rescue George Washington's portrait in
Flames in the city
A Tale of the War of 1812
October 2008

For more information visit:
timespies.com

Endless Quest

Thrilling adventures that let you control the story!

Claw of the Dragon
January 2008

Search for the Pegasus
July 2008

Lair of the Lich
December 2008

More choices to come in 2009!